A Pillar Box Red Publication

we *love* you...

Jessie J

AN UNAUTHORISED
2012 ANNUAL

Written by Sarah Milne

Designed by Lucy Boyd

Contents

How It All Began

Jessie J was born as Jessica Ellen Cornish in Redbridge, the youngest of three sisters. While her elder siblings excelled at school, Jessie was always interested in performing, and describes herself as being a "little show off". Fame started early for her, and Jessie started appearing in TV commercials as a child.

While at school, there was one thing she was good at – singing. In fact she was so good at it, that an 11 year old Jessie got kicked out of the school choir for being too loud – some of the other children were upset that she was so good. Jessie was heartbroken. But luckily she wasn't put off singing, always practising in front of the mirror with a hairbrush, Jessie started a band with her two sisters called The Cornish Pasties.

A love of musical theatre led Jessie to audition for a part in Andrew Lloyd Webber's hit west end show, Whistle Down the Wind, and aged just 10, she found herself on the stage, and loving it, going to school through the day and performing at night.

Around this time, as well as great success, Jessie also had lots of personal issues – she was diagnosed with an irregular heartbeat and spent lots of her early years being treated at Great Ormond Street Hospital, and she even had a mini stroke when she was 18 – the experience led Jessie to write her first song, Big White Room, about a boy on her ward that sadly died. To this day, Jessie's condition means that she doesn't drink, smoke or even have any caffeine, and she has to watch her health very carefully.

Jessie then started going to the BRIT School for Performing Arts, where classmates included Adele, Katie Melua and Amy Winehouse, and she joined another girl band, Soul Deep.

Initially signing a record deal to Gut records, Jessie was shocked when the company went bust, but didn't stop to feel sorry for herself. A publishing contract with Sony soon followed and led Jessie to write many songs for global artists, including Miley Cyrus and Chris Brown. In fact 'Do It Like A Dude' was originally written for Rihanna, but Justin Timberlake and others encouraged her to release it for herself.

The rest, as they say, is history, and Jessie J (the J stands for whatever you want it to) continues to grow as an artist, and one of the exciting emerging British female singers of today. We look forward to many more years of her style, sass and songs...

Factfile

FULL NAME: Jessica Ellen Cornish

DATE OF BIRTH: 27 March 1988

DAY OF BIRTH: Sunday

BORN: Redbridge

STARSIGN: Aries

HEIGHT: 5'9

SIBLINGS: Two older sisters

SCHOOL: went to the BRIT School for Performing Arts

HAIR: Black

EYES: Brown

LIKES: Having fun, inspiring people and writing songs that have meaning

DISLIKES: Not standing out from the crowd

12

13

Stars JJ has Written for and Worked with

After Jessie's first record company went bust, her talents were spotted elsewhere and she became a songwriter for Sony. During this time she wrote hits for many of the world's top performance artists, and most of them became hits. Here's a few of the most famous people she's written for.

Miley Cyrus

The All-American teen queen and daughter of country legend Billy Ray had a hit in 2009 with 'Party in the USA', co-written by Jessie J. It is now one of the best-selling singles in the US, and had sold over 4.5 million copies by April 2011.

Chris Brown

After Chris's tour manager spotted Jessie J on YouTube, she was asked to be a supporting artist for the R&B star on his European tour, as well as helping pen some songs for him too.

Katy Perry

Jessie has recently been supporting Katy Perry on her hugely successful California Dreams tour.

Rihanna (almost)

Do It Like a Dude was originally heading for Rihanna's camp, but it is rumoured that Justin Timberlake, among others, persuaded Jessie to keep it for herself. We're sure glad she did!

Alicia Keys

Jessie was one of the writers on Alicia's song L.O.V.E, and Ms Keys is said to be a huge fan of Jessie's own work.

And the rest...

It is said that Jessie has also written a song that Christina Aguilera, Mary J Blige and Alicia Keys have all recorded, but never released, and that the song has come back to Jessie now – only time will tell if it's a hit for her.

Cyndi Lauper

The legendary 'Girls Just Wanna Have Fun' singer personally asked for Jessie to be a supporting artist on her 2008 tour of the UK.

Wordsearch

K	M	O	O	R	E	T	I	H	W	G	I	B	Z	P
T	A	F	B	A	Z	G	W	K	S	W	G	O	P	U
N	G	T	E	I	H	W	B	B	X	E	S	S	E	V
Z	L	S	Y	M	J	S	E	D	I	X	Y	U	Y	P
U	A	W	T	P	U	G	I	Q	K	G	D	R	R	L
M	S	B	H	Q	E	T	Z	N	L	Z	Z	Y	S	R
H	T	J	R	J	X	R	M	W	R	A	V	C	G	O
P	O	N	O	A	Q	W	R	W	A	O	H	Y	S	C
T	N	E	N	K	C	Q	K	Y	F	O	C	E	G	E
D	B	G	E	K	N	A	A	I	I	Q	X	L	A	R
R	U	R	G	H	H	E	D	R	T	V	A	I	W	A
N	R	P	R	I	C	E	T	A	G	V	M	M	F	D
B	Y	Z	R	B	R	E	D	V	B	U	P	F	C	F
N	K	Z	H	K	K	Z	O	U	F	R	I	C	M	M
W	U	Y	I	Z	J	S	A	R	D	X	A	S	M	O

Pricetag   **Glastonbury**   **Choir**

Cornish   **Katy Perry**   **Essex**

Abracadabra   **Throne**   **Dare**

Dude   **Big White Room**   **Miley Cyrus**

Solution on page 61

17

Discography

Jessie J first sprung onto the scene in 2010, but since then she has been kept busy, releasing an album and other singles, as well as touring and performing on the festival circuit. She's also said that in the last 6 years, she has written over 600 songs, so we can expect much more to come in the near future!

2010

SINGLE

Do It Like A Dude
Went Gold in UK and New Zealand –
reached number 2 in the UK charts

2011

ALBUM

Who You Are
Went Platinum in UK, top ten in UK, Australia, Canada, Ireland and new Zealand – reached number 11 in the US charts

SINGLES

Price Tag (featuring B.o.B)
Went straight in at number 1 on the UK charts, also reached the top spot in France, Ireland and New Zealand. Platinum in UK and New Zealand. Knocked off the number 1 spot in the UK by school friend Adele

Nobody's Perfect
Reached number 9 in the UK and Australian charts

DIGITAL ONLY SINGLES

Abracadabra; Mama Knows best; Rainbow; Stand Up have all charted in the UK charts in 2011, through digital downloads alone

SOUNDTRACKS

Sexy Silk and Who You Are both appeared in film soundtrack in 2010 – Easy A and Step Up 3D

Crossword

Solution on page 61

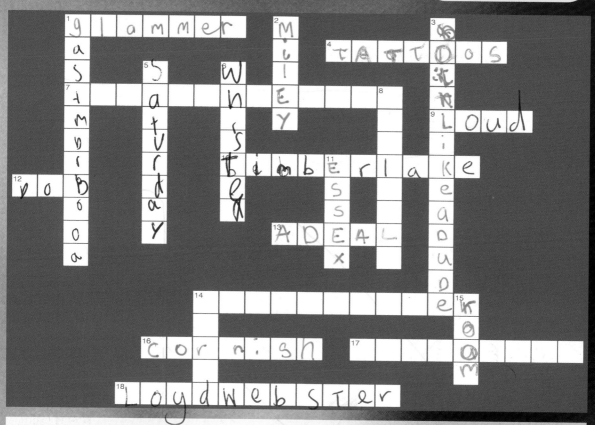

ACROSS

1 Jessie won the Woman of Tomorrow award from this magazine (7)

4 Jessie has four of these on her body – so far! (7)

7 That poker-straight hair would be nothing without a pair of these (13)

9 Jessie was kicked out of her school choir for being too what? (4)

10 This US star thinks Jessie is the greatest singer around just now - Justin _____ (10)

12 'Price Tag' featured this emerging artist (3)

13 School friend who rates Jessie's voice as so good it's "criminal" (5)

14 Jessie was the opening act for this 'Girls Just Wanna Have Fun' singer on her UK tour (5, 6)

16 Jessie's last name, also describes someone from Truro (7)

17 Debut album which took six years to finish (3, 3, 3)

18 Musical (see 6 Down) was a production by Andrew _____ (5, 6)

DOWN

1 Summer music festival where Jessie performed sitting on a throne in 2011 (11)

2 _____ Cyrus: Jessie wrote 'Party in the USA' for this singer (5)

3 Jessie's debut single, originally meant for Rihanna (2, 2, 4, 1, 4)

5 Jessie's first US TV appearance was on the legendary '_____ Night Live' (8)

6 '_____ Down the Wind' – Jessie appeared in this West End musical when she was just 10 (7)

8 Girl group Jessie was a part of at school (4, 4)

11 'The Only Way is _____' - where Jessie grew up (5)

14 Jessie shares a birthday with one of her idols, Mariah _____ (5)

15 The first song Jessie wrote, age 17, 'Big White _____ (4)

21

Other Famous Essex Faces

Jessie J was born in Essex, a place not always best known for being a hotbed of talent. But, you might be surprised when you read this list of fantastic other Essex girls (and boys)!

Jo Joyner, actress – the lovely Tanya Branning in Eastenders

Denise Van Outen, performer and presenter, now married to Lee Mead

Paul Danan, actor and reality show contestant

Anya Hindmarch, fashion designer and creator of "This is not a bag" bags

Dick Turpin, historical highwayman

Olly Murs, X Factor runner-up in 2009, and now a successful recording artist

Rupert Grint, Harry Potter actor, and unlikely heartthrob

Lauren Goodger, star of "The Only Way Is Essex"

Louie Spence, fabulous choreographer, star of Pineapple Dance Studios

Russell Brand, actor, comedian, writer and husband of Katy Perry

JJ Style

It's fair to say that Jessica Ellen Cornish (AKA Jessie J) really knows her own mind when it comes to style.

She once was asked whether she has a stylist, to which she replied:

"No. If someone did my make-up and my hair, and dressed me and wrote my songs I'm just being a dummy. If someone dressed me, I wouldn't feel like me"

So, it's clear that this is a girl who enjoys dressing up, and knows her own style, and she certainly likes to have fun with her image. Here's our guide to getting the Jessie J look.

The Hair

The poker straight bob with a heavy fringe is a key part of the Jessie J look – not easy to pull off for everyone, but her face shape and height (she's 5ft 9) means that she can wear it effortlessly. JJ says that she's had the same hair since she was little – sometimes she has it all tied back in a high ponytail too. At the 2011 Glamour Awards (where she won Woman of Tomorrow), Jessie tried a new, more ladylike do – a 40s style wave, with minimum makeup and an elegant floor length gown. We loved the change, but like Jessie's usual style better.

The Make-up

Apart from that award ceremony, Jessie doesn't normally go in for a natural look. Getting this right starts with striking eyes – strong eyebrows and kohled eyes and BIG lashes. Jessie usually finishes off with a brightly coloured lipstick, neon pink, bright red, black – whatever she feels like. Famously for promotional shots, Jessie's lips have been covered in studs/jewels and painted like a Union Jack.

The Clothes

Again, these are usually eye catching and fun. Lots of shorts and crop tops, showing off Jessie's great body. Patterned tights show off her long legs and fierce footwear usually finishes off the look. Not everyone can pull off an all-over body stocking, but she even managed to make that look great at the Brits 2011.

The Attitude

Being brave enough to wear what you want means being able to wear clothes and make-up that many others wouldn't. Jessie loves this aspect of her job, and tries not to take it all too seriously – it's just clothes, isn't it?

Jessie write?

3. Which famous school did Jessie go to, along with Adele and Amy Winehouse?

4. Why did Jessie perform sitting on a throne at Glastonbury 2011?

5. What chart position did debut single 'Do It Like A Dude' reach in the British charts?

6. Which show did Jessie make her American debut on?

7. Which of Jessie's tattoos helps her chill out when she looks at it?

8. Which other girl singer did Jessie J open for during a tour of America in 2011?

9. This famous ex-boy band singer encouraged Jessie J to release 'Do It Like A Dude'.

11. Jessie suffered one of these when performing in the dark in 2011.

12. How does Jessie like to spend her free time?

13. This female star thinks Jessie's voice is so good it's 'criminal'.

14. Jessie J's first number one single in the UK.

15. Jessie J asked fans to 'Dare' her on which website?

16. How tall is Jessie J?

17. What were Jessie's first words, lyrics from a 1990 hit song?

18. Jessie starred in this West End musical when she was just 10 year old.

19. What was the name of the first song Jessie wrote, aged 17?

20. This song title is also one of Jessie's tattoos, on her wrist.

Answers on page 60

Awards

As an emerging artist, Jessie J may not have the biggest list of awards (yet!), but the ones she has won are particularly important, and we're positive that there are many more to come. Many of the songs she's written for other artists are already winners, so it seems only fair that our girl shares in some of the glory.

2010

Jessie won the prestigious BBC Sound of 2011 award, an annual poll of music critics and industry figures to find the most promising new music talent. Previous winners include Adele, Ellie Goulding, 50 Cent and Mika.

2011 Brit Awards

Jessie J won the Critics' Choice award, another gong voted for by those in the know.

Dare Jessie J

Listening to the fans and getting feedback from them (good and bad) has always been important to Jessie, and at the end of 2010 fans got the chance to 'dare' their favourite star to do anything, and it could become an episode of a 12 part online TV show released on YouTube by MySpace Music.

Dare Jessie J allows fans to issue a series of challenges her way. Already those setting her tasks have included high profile fans Perez Hilton and Justin Timberlake. "Which is cool, of course it is, but I want everyone to get involved." Jessie has a democratic approach to her fans. "Just because someone's famous don't make them more important." The resulting TV show indicates just how fearless this incredible DIY pop star can be.

So far, the series has taken her to Trafalgar Square in a gorilla suit, bursting out into song in the middle of Time Square and travelling to Las Vegas and Los Angeles – is there nothing Jessie won't do?

What will you 'dare' Jessie to do next? Check out her MySpace page for the latest videos.

School Daze

When she was 16, Jessie started going to the BRIT school, which is dedicated to education and vocational training for the performing arts, media, art and design and the technologies that make performance possible. And it's pretty good at turning out performing stars. Here are some of the most famous BRIT alumni – can you imagine how good their school concert would have been?

Aggro Santos, Brazilian born rapper

Kate Nash: Singer/songwriter had a huge hit in 2007 with her song 'Foundations'

Blake Harrison: The Inbetweeners actor stars as the gormless Neil. A film is due to come out in 2011

Noisettes – singer Shingai and guitarist Dan met at the school

Amy Winehouse: The 'Rehab' singer was at the BRIT school as well as the Sylvia Young Theatre School

Richard Jones and Dan Sells of indie band The Feeling

Adele: Singer/songwriter was in the same year as Jessie J and they are still friends.

Dane Bowers – ex-boy band member and one of Katie Price's early boyfriends

Leona Lewis: X Factor winner in 2006, now a global recording artist

JJ Make-up

Jessie J is never a girl to be seen without some kind of make-up on, and like with her clothes, she likes to have fun with her looks, always trying different things. But, with such good skin and hair as well as a strong face shape, she can easily pull off bright colours.

Matching her clothes with her hair, Jessie is loving a bit of fluorescent at the moment – here, at a film premiere, she teams a hot cerise dress with the same shade of lipstick and strong eyes. We love the leopard print boots too – very feline.

Again, never afraid of colour, Jessie teams her strong fringe with well-shaped eyebrows framing dark eyes and those bright pink lips again – loving the splash of colour on her cheeks too.

JJ Influences

Music has always been an important part of Jessie's life. Her first words, aged just two, were "jam hot", a lyric from the hit 1990 song "Dub Be Good To Me", recently sampled by Professor Green and Lily Allen.

She may be a cool kid today, but when she was growing up, Jessie admits that it was her dad that was into cool music, playing music from 80s R&B stars D Train and funk legends Funkadelic while Jessie wanted to be in musical theatre.

But her dad's taste did rub off on her, and so Jessie's influences include Bob Marley, Aretha Franklin, Michael Jackson, and Prince. If she had to pick a musical idol it'd be between Whitney Houston and Mariah Carey and she also loves more up to date singers, like Kelly Rowland and Leona Lewis. There have been rumours of a Jessie/Leona Christmas single, but that's yet to be confirmed – watch this space!

And as for being a role model herself? Well Jessie has repeatedly said that she wants to be a positive influence on girls growing up, and certainly wants her music to say something meaningful, rather than just be a nice tune.

Name that Tune

Lyrics from JJ songs

"We need to take it
back in time,
when music made us all
_____Unite_____ "

"see love doesn't choose
a boy, or a girl, nope,
when I met you, you
_____hanged_____ my heart
and filled my world"

" Mama knows best
when times get hard, and
_____Dad_____ always has a
joke to make me laugh"

" Cause you're as old as you
feel you are, And if you don't
reach for the _____
you can't fall on the stars"

" Can I run more faster
than you, I wanna feel
my body again, feel the
_____ in my hair"

" The grass is _____
on the other side,
What I'm saying is
we're all alike"

"Coz you got my heart
_____, It's so
unreal you know,
Don't want this to stop"

" Cause love is a shield,
keeps us _____,
From what could
get even worse"

"So I sit and I realize,
With these tears falling
from my eyes,
I gotta change if I wanna
keep you _____ "

"Flyin, flying,
flying through the sky,
In my _____"

44

Solution on page 60

JJ Trivia

Jessie J has written songs for many huge stars like Chris Brown and Miley Cyrus.

Has four tattoos, including one with a spelling mistake (Says 'Don't loose who you are' instead of 'Don't lose who you are' – oops). Also has an image of a stick man and 'StandUp' on her wrist.

Is friends with Justin Timberlake, after meeting him at a studio.

Doesn't drink or smoke because of an irregular heartbeat.

Performed in the West End musical 'Whistle Down the Wind' for two years when she was just 10 years old!

Went to the same school as Adele, Amy Winehouse and Leona Lewis.

Was kicked out of her school choir for being too loud. She was only 11 years old!

Has written 600 songs in the last six years – phew!

Likes to hang out with friends who come over to play video games and eat spaghetti bolognese.

Her first words were 'jam hot', a lyric from the 1990 hit song 'Dub be Good to Me' (recently sampled by Professor Green and Lily Allen).

Say What?

Quotes by and about Jessie J

"I just want to change the world with my music."

JJ aims high

"I was in it for a day and some of the adults were moaning that their kids were upset that I was too good. I was 11. Can you imagine? I was heartbroken."

On being kicked out of the school choir for being too loud

"She's literally made normal artists and music boring, which bothers me. It annoys me when people say Leona Lewis is boring. No, she's not. She's got a sick voice and being normal is cool."

Jessie's thoughts on Lady Gaga

"the best singer in the world right now"

What Justin Timberlake thinks of Jessie J

"More than anything it shook me into a place where it doesn't matter how old you are, you have to get on with life and not take it for granted. It's helped me a lot on how I am as a person and my outlook on life."

On having a minor stroke when she was just 18

"No. If someone did my makeup and my hair, and dressed me and wrote my songs I'm just being a dummy. If someone dressed me, I wouldn't feel like me."

On whether she has a stylist

"I think it's important to be a role model and I'm very aware that a lot of young people look up to me. I feel it's my job to write emotional songs with substance that young people can relate to and learn from. I want to make music that makes everyone think."

On writing songs that really mean something

"I want to sit there with the Katy Perrys and the Gagas and the Rihannas and feel comfortable. I don't want to be the British chick who tried to make it and didn't. I'm not going to sleep until that happens."

Aiming high for the future

"I want to be at the top. I want to be a credible artist, not just someone here today and gone tomorrow. You're not going to get rid of me."

The future is bright for JJ

"I think her voice is illegal. The things she can do with her voice are criminal. I haven't heard many songs but I have seen acoustic performances online and she is like an acrobat or magician with her voice."

Former BRIT school alumnus Adele on Jessie's voice

Glastonbury

Despite injuring her foot earlier in the month, Jessie was a trooper and still wanted to play at Glastonbury. Doctors warned her to stay off her foot to allow it to heal properly, so what better way to perform than sitting on a throne? It certainly made sure that Jessie was crowned Queen of Glastonbury with fans and critics alike raving about her set. Maybe next time she'll get to walk about in the mud like everyone else!

The Future for JJ

At only 22 years old Jessie J has done pretty well for herself already, but we're sure there's lots more to come. Here's a few projects we think she'd be great at:

Start a fashion label. With such a great sense of style and a body to die for, Jessie could design and model her own creations – we'd definitely buy them!

Release an acoustic album. Maybe after the success of Who You Are, Jessie will change her sound? An unplugged feel may be the next step for her.

Become a make-up artist. Jessie loves messing around with her look, and her fierce make-up creations could be inspirational for other artists.

In an interview at the start of 2011, Jessie stated that her goals for the next twelve months are: have a number one album, go on a headline tour, launch a perfume, set up charities and youth clubs around London, write a musical, do a duet with Leona Lewis and write Britney Spears' next hit single. Sounds like she's going to have a busy time ahead!

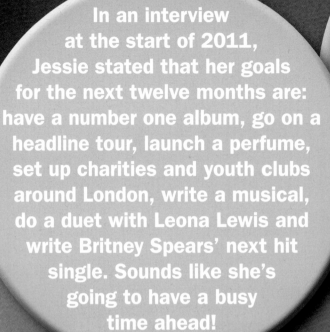

Writing more hit singles for global artists – we're sure Jessie would be a great writer for other strong women, like Gaga and Beyonce.

Become a teacher – Jessie has stated that she wants to be a positive role model for young girls, so what better way to inspire and educate the next generation?

On This Day

Jessie J was born on 27 March 1988, a Sunday. But what else has happened on that day in history? We pick out some of the more interesting facts about Jessie's birthday...

BIRTHDAYS
1863 – Sir Henry Royce (of Rolls Royce fame)
1886 – Famous architect Ludwig Mies van der Rohe
1922 – Author of Babe, Dick King-Smith
1963 – Director Quentin Tarantino
1970 – Performer and diva Mariah Carey
1971 – Formula 1 driver David Coulthard
1975 – Fergie from the Black Eyed Peas

1871
The first international rugby match, Scotland v England is played in Edinburgh. Scotland won.

1306
Robert the Bruce is crowned King of Scotland at Scone Palace.

27 March
is also World Theatre Day across the globe.

A-Z of JJ

A Adele – one of Jessie's school friends, Adele thinks JJ has a 'criminal' voice, it's so good.

B Brit School – where Jessie went, along with other great performers like Adele, Amy Winehouse and Katie Melua.

C Cornish – Jessie was born Jessica Ellen Cornish.

D Do It Like A Dude – debut single released in 2010.

E Essex girl – but, Jessie is less fake tan and hair extensions, more intelligence and sass.

F Fans – Jessie loves interacting with her fans through Twitter and MySpace.

G Glastonbury – Jessie played there in 2011, sitting on a throne to rest her injured foot.

H Hair – poker straight, glossy and fierce – we love the hair.

I Image – it's all her own style, and not made up by the record company.

J What does the J stand for? "Whatever you want it to"

K Katy Perry – JJ opened for Mrs Brand during her 2011 tour.

L Lips – Jessie loves experimenting with her make-up and to date her lips have been studded, jewelled and painted like the Union Jack.

M Miley Cyrus – JJ co-wrote her huge hit 'Party in the USA'

N Nobody's Perfect – third single from debut album 'Who You Are'

O On stage, Jessie is in her element – she loves performing live.

P Price Tag – second single went straight to number 1 in the UK charts.

Q Queen – Jessie was called the Queen of Glastonbury for performing through the pain of her injured foot.

R Rihanna – debut single 'Do It Like A Dude', was originally written for the Bajan diva.

S Show-off – Jessie admits she loved being the centre of attention, even from an early age.

T Justin Timberlake – the gorgeous Mr T encouraged JJ to start performing for herself, not writing for other people.

U Uncensored – Jessie J always speaks her mind.

V Volume – there's only one way to listen to JJ – turn it up!

W Woman of Tomorrow – Jessie was given this title at the Glamour Magazine Awards 2011.

X X Factor – Jessie has spoken about the talent show, saying that she would have felt like she had skipped the queue to success if she'd entered it.

Y Yellow – Jessie can even sport yellow eyeshadow and make it look cool!

Z Zzzs – because of her heart condition, Jessie has to make sure she gets enough sleep and doesn't party too much!

Quiz Answers

Name that Tune

"We need to take it back in time, when music made us all unite" (from Price Tag)

" Mama knows best when times get hard, and Papa always has a joke to make me laugh" (from Mama Knows Best)

" Can I run more faster than you, I wanna feel my body again, feel the wind in my hair" (from Big White Room)

"Coz you got my heart unlocked, It's so unreal you know, Don't want this to stop" (from Abracadabra)

"So I sit and I realize, With these tears falling from my eyes, I gotta change if I wanna keep you forever" (from Nobody's Perfect)

"see love doesn't choose a boy, or a girl, nope, when I met you, you hugged my heart and filled my world" (from L.O.V.E)

"Cause you're as old as you feel you are, And if you don't reach for the moon you can't fall on the stars" (from Stand Up)

"The grass is greener on the other side, What I'm saying is we're all alike" (from Rainbow)

"Cause love is a shield, keeps us concealed, From what could get even worse" (from Casualty of Love)

"Flyin, flying, flying through the sky, In my spaceship" (from Do It Like A Dude)

JJ Quiz

1. For being too loud!
2. Party in the USA
3. The BRIT School
4. Because her leg was in a plaster cast.
5. Number 2
6. Saturday Night Live
7. The stick man
8. Katy Perry
9. Justin Timberlake
10. Rihanna
11. Panic attack
12. Hanging out with friends, playing video games, eating spaghetti bolognese
13. Adele
14. Price Tag
15. Her MySpace page
16. 5ft 9'
17. "Jam Hot" , from 'Dub Be Good To Me'
18. Whistle Down The Wind
19. Big White Room
20. 'Stand Up"

Wordsearch

K	M	O	O	R	E	T	I	H	W	G	I	B	Z	P
T	A	F	B	A	Z	G	W	K	S	W	G	O	P	U
N	G	T	E	I	H	W	B	B	X	E	S	S	E	V
Z	L	S	Y	M	J	S	E	D	I	X	Y	U	Y	P
U	A	W	T	P	U	G	I	Q	K	G	D	R	R	L
M	S	B	H	Q	E	T	Z	N	L	Z	Z	Y	S	R
H	T	J	R	J	X	R	M	W	R	A	V	C	G	O
P	O	N	O	A	Q	W	R	W	A	O	H	Y	S	C
T	N	E	N	K	C	Q	K	Y	F	O	C	E	G	E
D	B	G	E	K	N	A	A	I	I	Q	X	L	A	R
R	U	R	G	H	H	E	D	R	T	V	A	I	W	A
N	R	P	R	I	C	E	T	A	G	V	M	M	F	D
B	Y	Z	R	B	R	E	D	V	B	U	P	F	C	F
N	K	Z	H	K	K	Z	O	U	F	R	I	C	M	M
W	U	Y	I	Z	J	S	A	R	D	X	A	S	M	O

Crossword

1. GLAMOUR
2. MILEY
3. DIT...
4. TATTOOS
5. SATURDAY
6. WHISTLE
7. STRAIGHTENERS
8. SOUSE...
9. LOUD
10. TIMBERLAKE
11. ...
12. BOB
13. ADELE
14. CYNDILAUPER
15. ROOM
16. CORNISH
17. WHOYOUARE
18. LLOYDWEBBER

Where's Jessie?